WIND SPINS ME AROUND IN THE FALL

WIND SPINS ME AROUND IN THE FALL

Charlotte Agell

Tilbury House, Publishers
Gardiner, Maine

To Aunt Nancy,
the inimitable

Tilbury House, Publishers
132 Water Street
Gardiner, ME 04345

First Printing

Agell, Charlotte.
    Wind spins me around in the Fall / Charlotte Agell.
       p.   cm.
    Summary: A little girl enjoys a full autumn day with her family, spinning in the leaves, watching the birds, and choosing pumpkins at a farm.
    ISBN 0-88448-114-X : $7.95
    [1. Autumn--Fiction.   2. Family life--Fiction.] I. Title.
PZ7.A2665Wi   1994
[E]--dc20
                                                                                            94-4866
                                                                                               CIP
                                                                                                AC

Designed by Edith Allard and Charlotte Agell
Editing and production: Mark Melnicove, Lisa Reece, Devon Phillips, and Lisa Holbrook
Office and warehouse: Jolene Collins

Imagesetting: High Resolution, Inc., Camden, Maine
Color separations: Graphic Color Service, Fairfield, Maine
Printing: Eusey Press, Leominster, Massachusetts
Binding: The Book Press, Brattleboro, Vermont

Leaves are falling,
wind is blowing,

I am flying!
Fall is here.

My aunt is visiting.

Surprise!

Whoosh! Crunch! Whirl!

Look, I am a bat.

The world looks funny upside down,
leaves fall up,
smoke flies down.

Tickle, tickle,
teases my aunt.

We go
spin — spin — spinning
in the wind

until we fall
in the crispy leaves
near the noisy birds
in the hawthorn tree.

The grosbeaks are flocking,
getting ready to fly south,
says my aunt.

But I think they are having
a bird tea party.
I want a snack, too!

Now my belly is full,
but our bird feeder is empty.

The chickadees don't mind me,
but the finches hide in the bush.

Back indoors, mama says,
"Time to go buy pumpkins!"

Leaves blow right in the door.
"It is a busy time of year for brooms,"
says papa.

Swish — swish — swish.
I am sailing on a yellow ocean

all the way to the farm.
Hurrah!

The big dog barks,
but mama says she is friendly.

There are papa pumpkins,
mama pumpkins, and baby pumpkins.
"Aunt pumpkins, too," says my aunt.

This grandma pumpkin
is too big for our wagon.

We choose a family of pumpkins
to take home.

I am so excited
I hug papa's leg.

"I am not your papa,"
smiles the farmer.
"But thanks for the hug."

The sun is sinking
like a giant pumpkin.

At home, I draw a face
with a grin.

Mama carves our jack-o-lantern.
Papa saves some seeds
for planting in the spring.

Night falls before supper
in the fall.
I am extra hungry!

I wish the sky
was a bowl full of stars,

and the moon,
my spoon.

Other books in this series by Charlotte Agell

MUD MAKES ME DANCE IN THE SPRING
I WEAR LONG GREEN HAIR IN THE SUMMER
I SLIDE INTO THE WHITE OF WINTER

For more information, write or call:
Tilbury House, Publishers
132 Water Street, Gardiner, ME 04345
1-800-582-1899; fax 207-582-8227